For Joseph and Elizabeth Garner
W.M.

For Bella
P.B.

Copyright © 1984 by William Mayne
Illustrations copyright © 1984 by Patrick Benson
First published in the United States of America
in 1984 by Philomel Books,
a member of The Putnam Publishing Group,
51 Madison Avenue, New York, NY 10010
First published 1984 by
Walker Books Ltd, London
Printed and bound in Italy. All rights reserved.

Library of Congress Cataloging in Publication Data
Mayne, William
The red book of Hob stories.
Summary: Five episodes featuring Hob,
a goblin, and the family he lives with and
protects, though only the children can see him.
[1. Fairies—Fiction] I. Benson, Patrick, ill.
II. Title. III. Title: Hob stories.
PZ7.M4736RE 1984 [Fic] 83-15125
ISBN 0-399-21047-4

THE RED BOOK OF
HOB
STORIES

WILLIAM MAYNE

ILLUSTRATED BY PATRICK BENSON

PHILOMEL BOOKS
New York

HOB AND BOGGART

Who lit a twiggy fire in the ashes of the hearth and filled the house with smoke in the middle of the night?

Mr. asks the question, Mrs. wants to know. Boy and Girl did not do it and cannot tell.

Budgie, the pet bird, knows. Baby sees and yells the name, but no one understands.

"We'll go back to bed," says Mr. "I hope it's not your friend."

Boy and Girl know kindly Hob lives in his cutch or cupboard underneath the stairs. They know he did no such thing.

"No," says Hob. "But I'm about. Hob is where he thinks he is."

Mr. and Mrs. and Boy and Girl go back to bed.

"I saw it, I saw it," says Budgie.

Hop jumps up and makes a face at her. He thinks Budgie is a noise and not a thing. He is quiet himself and does not like a noise.

"Who is it?" he asks. But Budgie tucks her head under her wing and will not reply.

Hob goes to ask Baby.

"Wug, wug, wug," says Baby. Only Baby understands. Hob makes a face at it, and Baby laughs. Hob goes to find out for himself.

He listens. Something bumps about the house. Hob hears the milk go sour. Something rattles at a door. Hob hears the bread go moldy. Something shuffles across a floor. Hob hears the butter going wrong. Treading down the stairs he hears a scratching down below. There is something climbing into his cutch, his living place.

Hob is angry now. He goes right down. He thinks

he knows what this thing is. Budgie has fainted quite away, her feathers turning white. "It made a face at me," she croaks.

"It's one of those," says Hob.

"Hob thinks we'll have a fight."

There, climbing into the cutch, is a fat and ugly Boggart with really wicked eyes, bringing trouble and noise to Hob's own lucky house.

"Goodnight, Hob," says Boggart. "You'll have to move."

But Hob knows how to deal with Boggart. "We're all off," he says, cheerfully. "We're flitting, moving, don't you know. We're doing it to trick you."

"Silly Hob to tell me, then," says Boggart, climbing out. "Where do we go?"

"Wait a bit," says Hob, and out he goes for a wheelbarrow and puts a box on it. "Room for you in here," says Hob, and Boggart clambers in, mean and greedy. Hob wheels him away.

"What a trick," says Boggart. "They don't want me and here I am."

"What a trick," says Hob. "Here we are," and tips the barrow in the river, box, Boggart, and all, and they float away. "Wet house," says Boggart, and Hob says, "Goodbye."

Hob goes home to see what Boy and Girl had left him. He hopes it is not clothes, or he will have to go. "If they cover Hob's back, He's off down the track," he says. But they left a twist of baccy. He smokes it by the chimney.

"Home, sweet home," he says, among kindly folk.

HOB AND NOBODY

"It is a lucky house," says Mr., coming down the morning stairs.

"A happy house," says Mrs.

"We like it here," say Boy and Girl. "And we know why." They know that friendly Hob lives underneath the stairs in a little cutch or cupboard.

"What nonsense then," says Mr. "Now where are my vest and my hat? Who has seen them?"

Nobody has seen them.

"And where are my apron and the tea cozy?" says

Mrs. "Who has moved them?"

Nobody has moved them.

"And where," says Boy, "are my soccer boots and my satchel?"

Nobody has touched them.

"And where are my ribbons and my skipping rope?" says Girl.

Nobody knows.

Baby calls out for his bottle.

Nobody hears.

Hob in his cutch fast asleep wakes up and wonders. "Hob has heard," he says. "Hob and Nobody. Nobody knows better, and Nobody knows worse."

Mr. finds his vest and his hat.

Mrs. finds her apron and the tea cozy.

Boy finds his soccer boots and his satchel.

Girl finds her ribbons and her skipping rope.

They have all been put tidy by the fireside.

"Mischief did that," says Mr., looking at Boy and Girl.

"Nobody knows," says Mrs.

"Nobody cares," says Budgie in her cage.

"Nobody won't give me my bottle," says Baby in his cradle, and Nobody understands him, or Budgie.

Hob looks from his spyhole in the side of the cutch. "I wish Hob was more real," he says. "I'd go down and talk to them. But tonight I'll tell Nobody not  to do it. This is meant to be a lucky house."

Mr. dresses in his vest and his hat; Mrs. puts on her apron and makes the tea. Boy goes to school with his

boots, and Girl with her ribbons. Baby kicks in the cradle.

That night they are asleep when Hob comes out. He looks for Nobody. He knows what Nobody did. Nobody gave him clothes, vest, apron, boots, ribbons.

"Nobody wants Hob to go away," says Hob. He knows what he knows. "Hob on the road begging a lift, Things to wear are a parting gift."

He finds Nobody in the dark, putting things in the wrong places. "Hey, Nobody," says Hob.

"Mr. Nobody," says Nobody. "If you please."

"Mr. Nobody, come with me," says Hob. "I'll find a happy nowhere place for you." And Hob puts him where Nobody goes, in the corners of the loft, down the sides of chairs, behind the watertank. Nobody doesn't mind spiders.

"There," says Hob. Budgie is so glad she claps hands and falls off her perch.

"Hob is the lucky one," says Hob, and drinks the milk Boy and Girl leave for him. "Hob is lucky. This is home."

HOB AND THE BLACK HOLE

Girl sits down to do her darning. "My heels and toes came through," she says. She sits on sleeping Hob in a chair by the fire. "Oh Hob, I'm sorry," says Girl. "It is too dark to see you."

"Do your work and don't pretend," says Mrs. "There's such a lot to mend just now."

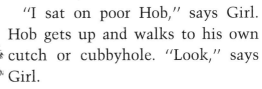

"I sat on poor Hob," says Girl. Hob gets up and walks to his own cutch or cubbyhole. "Look," says Girl.

"I can't see that," says Mrs. And then they mend and darn.

Hob gets into his cutch. He slept in the chair because the cutch is drafty. There is a hole in the wall, not his eyehole spyhole, but a big and cold one. He shivers.

Mr. says, "There's a round hole in the window, very strange."

Boy says, "There's water in my shoe, a hole in the sole."

"There's something about," says Hob. "Hob knows the signs." He closes his eyes until night.

Then something crawls up to Budgie. Budgie worries. She can't see it. "It's trying to get into the cage," she squeals.

"It can have you," says Hob.

Budgie rings her bell and he has to go to help. There is something on the cage. Hob cannot see it either. He can only see there's nothing there. There is an empty space. The empty space is sucking up Budgie's seeds.

"What are you doing here?" Hob asks. "Hob wants to know."

"Don't talk," says Budgie. "Peck it to death."

"I'm lost," says the thing. "I'm a baby black hole. I can't eat hard things like Mummy can, and I feel ill, and I want to go home."

"No wonder you feel ill," says Hob. "You have been eating toes of socks and soles of shoes."

"I was lying on the floor," says the baby black hole.

"On your way up here you ate the side of my cutch,"

says Hob. "But come with me. We'll find your Mummy."

Very carefully he picks the baby black hole from the side of the cage. If a black hole nips you that piece has gone for ever. He takes it outside in the night, and the baby black hole looks at the big black sky.

"Mummy," it calls. "I see you, all that black."

But a star comes out, so Mummy is not there; and another comes, and she is not there either; and more and more. The baby black hole cries a little tear into itself. And all the sky comes bright. Except for one dark corner. And that corner comes nearer and closer and picks up the baby black hole, and off they go together, Mummy black hole and baby black hole.

Hob goes in and counts himself. He is all there. Black holes never leave you a present. But Boy and Girl have left him a piece of wood to mend his cutch. "Can't eat it," says Hob. "But I'm not hungry, somehow," and off he goes to bed with it.

HOB AND THE SAD

Who sent a card to Hob one winter, in snow, when Christmas comes to people? Was it friend Lob?

"Does Hob live here?" the postman asks.

"Yes," say Boy and Girl.

"What nonsense then," says Mr.

Mrs. says the children have their fun, and Baby says "Happy Bubble" and Budgie sings a carol.

Boy puts the card for Hob in Hob's place, his cutch or den. He sleeps by day and keeps the house by night.

"Well," says Hob when he wakes up, "Time has remembered me," and reads his card to Budgie. It is all Hobbish words. Budgie sings Budgie words to Hob.

Hob goes to see what has gone on that day. He finds parcels not for him. He finds trimmings on a tree, paper chains across the room,
and holly by the wall.

"Give us a kiss," says Budgie,
underneath the mistletoe.

Hob makes a face at her. He is
looking for something that should

be there. The people had been nearly happy as they made Christmas ready, but not quite so. Something had been sad.

Hob finds the Sad. It is hiding by the fireside, a miserable lump, padding up and down on four small legs.

"I feel so flat," it says. "So sad. It's my work, I know, but I don't like it."

"Tell Hob what it has to do," says Hob. "Hob has to know."

"Oh, oh, oh," says the Sad. "Look on the table."

"I see there flour and milk, egg and sugar, yeast and fat and currants. That's work for Hob to do. By the fire they leave rewards. Hob don't care for salt and stitches, He's off in a moment if you give him britches. I see an egg on the table. It's not for him, but Hob loves an egg."

"It's all for me," says Sad. "I make bread hard and cake sink in the middle, and nothing will cure me."

"Tomorrow they have Christmas," says Hob. "Have you tried dancing, little Sad?"

"I tread on my own feet," says Sad.

"Have you sung a song?"

"Yes, but I bit my tongue."

Hob climbs to his cutch. He brings out a wooden flute and a wooden spoon. First he takes the wooden spoon. This is his work. He mixes egg and milk and sugar, yeast and flour, fat and fruit.

"A waste of time," says Sad.

"Time sent me a card," says Hob. "Jump in, Sad, my stirring's nearly done."

Sad holds his breath and tumbles in.

"I'll spoil your work," he says.

Hob plays the flute. The dough moves and rises, lifts itself and swings about.

"Oh, I am charmed," says Sad, "I am cured," and the dough comes high in the bowl and smiles.

Hob pops it in the oven to be ready in the morning. "They'll want a turkey too," he says to Budgie, who sulks at him.

Hob has his reward, a stocking with an apple. He reads his card. It says, "Happy wishes Hob New Year."

HOB AND BLACK DOG

Girl keeps her room tidy, sweeps her floor, washes her face. She finds sixpence in her shoe.

"It's my reward for being clean," she says. "I got it from our Hob."

"Someone dropped it, I dare say," says Mr.

Mrs. says, "Children love a game."

Hob says, "Hob's turn to give rewards."

"Hob will have a present specially from me," says Girl. "I'll make it or I'll buy."

Hob hopes she does not make mistakes and give him clothes to wear. If she did he would have to leave. He likes to live and work here.

"Dress him and he leaves his labor, Hob will find another neighbor," says Hob.

Budgie says, "Goodbye, perhaps."

Boy comes in with stray Black Dog. "I found him walking down the path," he says. "He has no collar, no tag, no home."

Black Dog licks his hand. Black Dog will not come near the fire.

"Hob wonders why," says Hob.

Budgie sings, "Perhaps it's Lob."

Hob looks again. "Lob is black," he says, "but Lob is Hob's friend. I think this is Black Dog."

Black Dog stays in a shadow. He looks. He stares. Mrs. says he ought to go outside. But Black Dog sits and looks.

"Black Dog has got in," says Hob. "Hob will think."

Black Dog will not eat or drink. He will not go out.

"I wish I had not brought him in," says Boy. "But he walked so quietly along with me, so lost."

Black Dog lies in the shadows under the table.

"He should be in a kennel," says Mrs.

"Hob isn't sure of that," says Hob.

Black Dog licks Girl's hand. "What a dry lick," says Girl. "In the dark I almost see through him."

Black Dog is a pair of eyes. He looks at everyone. Budgie is so alarmed she puts her head in the waterpot.

"There's dogs and Dogs," says Hob. "Black and Blacker."

The people go to bed. Black Dog stays under the table.

"Leave it to Hob," says Girl.

"Leave it to Hob," says Boy.

"Leave it to Hob," says Hob. Hob sets to work. It is not hard for him. He takes a strap and makes a collar. He has another sixpence and he hangs that on. Then he puts the collar on Black Dog. Black Dog licks Hob, blinks his eyes, and says that now he's dressed he'll go.

"It's the same for you as it is for Hob," says Hob.

Hob opens the door. Black Dog goes to do his work, to help people cross the street, to make sure they find their way, to keep travelers safe in rocky places.

"That's that," says Hob, shutting the door. "Come out, Budgie."

Budgie comes out. Budgie barks.

"Just like home," says Hob. He finds the reward Girl left him, a candy stick. He takes it to his cutch or den to eat it. In the house there are only shadows with no eyes.